the nursery 'ALICE'

[*See p.* 50.

Lewis Carroll's

the nursery 'ALICE'

Adapted from
"ALICES ADVENTURES IN WONDERLAND"
by *LEWIS CARROLL*
Colour illustrations by *TENNIEL*

OMEGA

This edition published in 1985 by Omega Books Limited,
1 West Street, Ware, Hertfordshire.

ISBN No: 1 85007 051 2

Printed and bound in Hong Kong by South China Printing Co.

A Nursery Darling.

A Mother's breast:
Safe refuge from her childish fears,
From childish troubles, childish tears,
Mists that enshroud her dawning years!
See how in sleep she seems to sing
A voiceless psalm — an offering
Raised, to the glory of her King,
In Love: for Love is Rest.

A Darling's kiss:
Dearest of all the signs that fleet
From lips that lovingly repeat
Again, again, their message sweet!
Full to the brim with girlish glee,
A child, a very child is she,
Whose dream of Heaven is still to be
At Home: for Home is Bliss.

PREFACE.

(ADDRESSED TO ANY MOTHER.)

I HAVE reason to believe that "Alice's Adventures in Wonderland" has been read by some hundreds of English Children, aged from Five to Fifteen: also by Children, aged from Fifteen to Twenty-five: yet again by Children, aged from Twenty-five to Thirty-five: and even by Children —— for there *are* such —— Children in whom no waning of health and strength, no weariness of the solemn mockery, and the gaudy glitter, and the hopeless misery, of Life has availed to parch the pure fountain of joy that wells up in all child-like hearts —— Children of a "certain" age, whose tale of years must be left untold, and buried in respectful silence.

And my ambition *now* is (is it a vain one?) to be read by Children aged from Nought to Five. To be read? Nay, not so!

PREFACE *(continued).*

Say rather to be thumbed, to be cooed over, to be dogs'-eared, to be rumpled, to be kissed, by the illiterate, ungrammatical, dimpled Darlings, that fill your Nursery with merry uproar, and your inmost heart of hearts with a restful gladness!

Such, for instance, as a child I once knew, who —— having been carefully instructed that *one* of any earthly thing was enough for any little girl; and that to ask for *two* buns, *two* oranges, *two* of anything, would certainly bring upon her the awful charge of being "greedy"—— was found one morning sitting up in bed, solemnly regarding her *two* little naked feet, and murmuring to herself, softly and penitently, "deedy!"

Easter-tide, 1890.

C O N T E N T S.

I.

THE WHITE RABBIT.

ONCE upon a time, there was a little girl called Alice: and she had a very curious dream.

Would you like to hear what it was that she dreamed about?

Well, this was the *first* thing that happened. A White Rabbit came running by, in a great hurry; and, just as it passed Alice, it stopped, and took its watch out of its pocket.

Wasn't *that* a funny thing? Did *you* ever see a Rabbit that had a watch, and a pocket to put it in? Of course, when a Rabbit has a watch, it *must* have a pocket to put it in: it would never do to carry it about in its mouth ——and it wants its hands sometimes, to run about with.

Hasn't it got pretty pink eyes (I think *all* White Rabbits have pink eyes); and pink ears; and a nice brown coat; and you can just see its red pocket-handkerchief peeping out of its coat-pocket: and, what with its blue neck-tie and its yellow waistcoat, it really is *very* nicely dressed.

"Oh dear, oh dear!" said the Rabbit. "I shall be too late!" *What* would it be too late *for*, I wonder? Well, you see, it had to go and visit the Duchess (you'll see a picture of the Duchess, soon, sitting in her kitchen): and the Duchess was a very cross old lady: and the Rabbit *knew* she'd be very angry indeed if he kept her waiting. So the poor thing was as frightened as frightened could be (Don't you see how he's trembling? Just shake the book a little, from side to side, and you'll soon see him tremble), because he thought the Duchess would have his head cut off, for a punishment. That was what the Queen of Hearts used to do, when *she* was angry with people (you'll see a picture of *her,* soon) : at least she used to *order* their heads to be cut off, and she always *thought* it was done, though they never *really* did it.

And so, when the White Rabbit ran away, Alice wanted to see what would happen to it : so she ran after it : and she ran, and she ran, till she tumbled right down the rabbit-hole.

And then she had a very long fall indeed. Down, and down, and down, till she began to wonder if she was going right *through* the World, so as to come out on the other side !

It was just like a very deep well : only there was no water in it. If anybody *really* had such a fall as that, it would kill them, most likely : but you know it doesn't hurt a bit to fall in a *dream,* because, all the time you *think* you're falling, you really *are* lying somewhere, safe and sound, and fast asleep !

However, this terrible fall came to an end at last, and down came Alice on a heap of sticks and dry leaves. But she wasn't a bit hurt, and up she jumped, and ran after the Rabbit again.

And so that was the beginning of Alice's curious dream. And, next time you see a White Rabbit, try and fancy *you're* going to have a curious dream, just like dear little Alice.

II.

HOW ALICE GREW TALL.

AND so, after Alice had tumbled down the rabbit-hole, and had run a long long way underground, all of a sudden she found herself in a great hall, with doors all round it.

But all the doors were locked: so, you see, poor Alice couldn't get out of the hall: and that made her very sad.

However, after a little while, she came to a little table, all made of glass, with three legs (There are *two* of the legs in the picture, and just the *beginning* of the other leg, do you see?), and on the table was a little key: and she went round the hall, and tried if she could unlock any of the doors with it.

Poor Alice! The key wouldn't unlock *any* of the doors. But at last she came upon a tiny little door: and oh, how glad she was, when she found the key would fit it!

So she unlocked the tiny little door, and she stooped down and looked through it, and what do you think she saw? Oh, such a beautiful garden! And she did so *long* to go into it! But the door was *far* too small. She couldn't squeeze herself through, any more than *you* could squeeze yourself into a mouse-hole!

So poor little Alice locked up the door, and took the key back to the table again: and *this* time she found quite a new thing on it (now look at the picture again), and what do you think it was? It was a little bottle, with a label tied to it, with the words "DRINK ME" on the label.

So she tasted it : and it was *very* nice : so she set to work, and drank it up. And then *such* a curious thing happened to her! You'll never guess what it was : so I shall have to tell you. She got smaller, and smaller, till at last she was just the size of a little doll!

Then she said to herself "*Now* I'm the right size to get through the little door!" And away she ran. But, when she got there, the door was locked, and the key was on the top of the table, and she couldn't reach it! *Wasn't* it a pity she had locked up the door again?

Well, the next thing she found was a little cake : and it had the words "EAT ME" marked on it. So of course she set to work and ate it up. And *then* what do you think happened to her? No, you'll never guess! I shall have to tell you again.

She grew, and she grew, and she grew. Taller than she was before! Taller than *any* child! Taller than any grown-up person! Taller,

and taller, and taller!
Just look at the picture,
and you'll *see* how tall
she got!

Which would *you*
have liked the best, do
you think, to be a little
tiny Alice, no larger than
a kitten, or a great tall
Alice, with your head
always knocking against
the ceiling?

III.

THE POOL OF TEARS.

PERHAPS you think Alice must have been very much pleased, when she had eaten the little cake, to find herself growing so tremendously tall? Because of course it would be easy enough, *now*, to reach the little key off the glass table, and to open the little tiny door.

Well, of course she could do *that*: but what good was it to get the door open, when she couldn't get *through*? She was worse off than ever, poor thing! She could just manage, by putting her head down, close to the ground, to *look* through with one eye! But that was *all* she could do. No wonder the poor tall child sat down and cried as if her heart would break.

So she cried, and she cried. And her tears ran down the middle of the hall, like a deep

c

river. And very soon there was quite a large Pool of Tears, reaching half-way down the hall.

And there she might have staid, till this very day, if the White Rabbit hadn't happened to come through the hall, on his way to visit the Duchess. He was dressed up as grand as grand could be, and he had a pair of white kid gloves in one hand, and a little fan in the other hand: and he kept on muttering to himself. "Oh, the Duchess, the Duchess! Oh, *won't* she be savage if I've kept her waiting!"

But he didn't see Alice, you know. So, when she began to say "If you please, Sir ——" her voice seemed to come from the top of the hall, because her head was so high up. And the Rabbit was dreadfully frightened: and he dropped the gloves and the fan, and ran away as hard as he could go.

Then a *very* curious thing indeed happened. Alice took up the fan, and began to fan herself with it: and, lo and behold, she got quite small again, and, all in a minute, she was just about the size of a mouse!

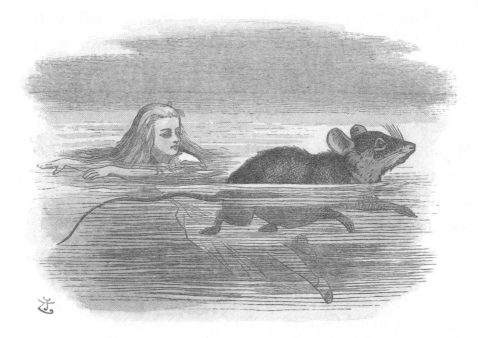

Now look at the picture, and you'll soon guess what happened next. It looks just like the sea, doesn't it? But it *really* is the Pool of Tears —— all made of *Alice's* tears, you know!

And Alice has tumbled into the Pool: and the Mouse has tumbled in: and there they are, swimming about together.

Doesn't Alice look pretty, as she swims across the picture? You can just see her blue stockings, far away under the water.

But why is the Mouse swimming away from Alice in such a hurry? Well, the reason is, that Alice began talking about cats and dogs: and a Mouse always *hates* talking about cats and dogs!

Suppose *you* were swimming about, in a Pool of your own Tears: and suppose somebody began talking to *you* about lesson-books and bottles of medicine, wouldn't *you* swim away as hard as you could go?

IV.

THE CAUCUS-RACE.

WHEN Alice and the Mouse had got out of the Pool of Tears, of course they were very wet: and so were a lot of other curious creatures, that had tumbled in as well. There was a Dodo (that's the great bird, in front, leaning on a walking-stick); and a Duck; and a Lory (that's just behind the Duck, looking over its head); and an Eaglet (that's on the left-hand side of the Lory); and several others.

Well, and so they didn't know how in the world they were to get dry again. But the Dodo —— who was a very wise bird —— told them the right way was to have a Caucus-Race. And what do you think *that* was?

You don't know? Well, you *are* an ignorant child! Now, be very attentive, and I'll soon cure you of your ignorance!

First, you must have a *racecourse*. It ought to be a *sort* of circle, but it doesn't much matter *what* shape it is, so long as it goes a good way round, and joins on to itself again.

Then, you must put all the *racers* on the course, here and there : it doesn't matter *where*, so long as you don't crowd them too much together.

Then, you needn't say "One, two, three, and away!" but let them all set off running just when they like, and leave off just when they like.

So all these creatures, Alice and all, went on running round and round, till they were all quite dry again. And then the Dodo said *everybody* had won, and *everybody* must have prizes!

Of course *Alice* had to give them their prizes. And she had nothing to give them but a few comfits she happened to have in her pocket. And there was just one a-piece, all round. And there was no prize for Alice!

So what do you think they did? Alice had nothing left but her thimble. Now look at the picture, and you'll see what happened.

"Hand it over here!" said the Dodo.

Then the Dodo took the thimble and handed it back to Alice, and said "We beg your acceptance of this elegant thimble!" And then all the other creatures cheered.

Wasn't *that* a curious sort of present to give her?   Suppose they wanted to give *you* a birth-day-present, would you rather they should go to your toy-cupboard, and pick out your nicest doll, and say "Here, my love, here's a lovely birthday-present for you!" or would you like them to give you something *new*, something that *didn't* belong to you before?

V.

BILL, THE LIZARD.

Now I'm going to tell you about Alice's Adventures in the White Rabbit's house.

Do you remember how the Rabbit dropped his gloves and his fan, when he was so frightened at hearing Alice's voice, that seemed to come down from the sky? Well, of course he couldn't go to visit the Duchess *without* his gloves and his fan: so, after a bit, he came back again to look for them.

By this time the Dodo and all the other curious creatures had gone away, and Alice was wandering about all alone.

So what do you think he did? Actually he thought she was his housemaid, and began

D

ordering her about! "Mary Ann!" he said. "Go home this very minute, and fetch me a pair of gloves and a fan! Quick, now!"

Perhaps he couldn't see very clearly with his pink eyes: for I'm sure Alice doesn't look very *like* a housemaid, *does* she? However she was a very good-natured little girl: so she wasn't a bit offended, but ran off to the Rabbit's house as quick as she could.

It was lucky she found the door open: for, if she had had to ring, I suppose the *real* Mary Ann would have come to open the door: and she would *never* have let Alice come in. And I'm sure it was *very* lucky she didn't meet the real Mary Ann, as she trotted upstairs: for I'm afraid she would have taken Alice for a robber!

So at last she found her way into the Rabbit's room: and there was a pair of gloves lying on the table, and she was just going to take them up and go away, when she happened to see a little bottle on the table. And of course it had the words "DRINK ME!" on the label. And of course Alice drank some!

Well, I think that was *rather* lucky, too : don't *you?* For, if she *hadn't* drunk any, all this wonderful adventure, that I'm going to tell you about, wouldn't have happened at all. And wouldn't *that* have been a pity?

You're getting so used to Alice's Adventures, that I daresay you can guess what happened next? If you can't, I'll tell you.

She grew, and she grew, and she grew. And in a very short time the room was full of *Alice :* just in the same way as a jar is full of jam! There was *Alice* all the way up to the ceiling : and *Alice* in every corner of the room!

The door opened inwards : so of course there wasn't any room to open it : so when the Rabbit got tired of waiting, and came to fetch his gloves for himself, of course he couldn't get in.

So what do you think he did? (Now we come to the picture). He sent Bill, the Lizard, up to the roof of the house, and told him to get down the chimney. But Alice happened to have one of her feet in the fire-place : so, when she heard Bill coming down the chimney, she just gave a little tiny kick, and away went Bill, flying up into the sky!

Poor little Bill! Don't you pity him very much? How frightened he must have been!

VI.

THE DEAR LITTLE PUPPY.

WELL, it doesn't look such a very *little* Puppy, does it? But then, you see, Alice had grown very small indeed : and *that's* what makes the Puppy look so large. When Alice had eaten one of those little magic cakes, that she found in the White Rabbit's house, it made her get quite small, directly, so that she could get through the door : or else she could *never* have got out of the house again. Wouldn't *that* have been a pity? Because then she wouldn't have dreamed all the other curious things that we're going to read about.

So it really *was* a *little* Puppy, you see. And isn't it a little *pet*? And look at the way it's barking at the little stick that Alice is holding out for it! You can see she was a *little* afraid of it, all the time, because she's got behind that great thistle, for fear it should run over her. That would have been just about as bad, for *her*, as it would be for *you* to be run over by a waggon and four horses!

Have you got a little pet puppy at *your* home? If you have, I hope you're always kind to it, and give it nice things to eat.

Once upon a time, I knew some little children, about as big as you; and they had a little pet dog of their own; and it was called *Dash*. And this is what they told me about its birthday-treat.

"Do you know, one day we remembered it was Dash's birthday that day. So we said 'Let's give Dash a nice birthday-treat, like what we have on *our* birthdays!' So we thought and we thought 'Now, what is it *we* like best of all, on *our* birthdays?' And we thought and we thought. And at last we all called out together 'Why, its *oatmeal-porridge*, of course!' So of

course we thought Dash would be *quite* sure to like it very much, too.

"So we went to the cook, and we got her to make a saucerful of nice oatmeal - porridge. And then we called Dash into the house, and we said 'Now, Dash, you're going to have your birthday-treat!' We expected Dash would jump for joy : but it didn't, one bit!

"So we put the saucer down before it, and we said 'Now, Dash, don't be greedy! Eat it nicely, like a good dog!'

"So Dash just tasted it with the tip of its tongue : and then it made, oh, such a horrid face! And then, do you know, it did *hate* it so, it wouldn't eat a bit more of it! So we had to put it all down its throat with a spoon!"

I wonder if Alice will give *this* little Puppy some porridge? I don't think she *can*, because she hasn't got any with her. I can't see any saucer in the picture.

VII.

THE BLUE CATERPILLAR.

WOULD you like to know what happened to Alice, after she had got away from the Puppy? It was far too large an animal, you know, for *her* to play with. (I don't suppose *you* would much enjoy playing with a young Hippopotamus, would you? You would always be expecting to be crushed as flat as a pancake under its great heavy feet!) So Alice was very glad to run away, while it wasn't looking.

Well, she wandered up and down, and didn't know what in the world to do, to make herself grow up to her right size again. Of course she knew that she had to eat or drink *something:* that was the regular rule, you know: but she couldn't guess *what* thing.

E

However, she soon came to a great mushroom, that was so tall that she couldn't see over
the top of it without standing on tip-toe.   And
what do you think she saw?   Something that
I'm sure *you* never talked to, in all your life!

It was a large Blue Caterpillar.

I'll tell you, soon, what Alice and the Caterpillar talked about : but first let us have a good look at the picture.

That curious thing, standing in front of the Caterpillar, is called a "hookah": and it's used for smoking. The smoke comes through that long tube, that winds round and round like a serpent.

And do you see its long nose and chin? At least, they *look* exactly like a nose and chin, don't they? But they really *are* two of its legs. You know a Caterpillar has got *quantities* of legs: you can see some more of them, further down.

What a bother it must be to a Caterpillar, counting over such a lot of legs, every night, to make sure it hasn't lost any of them!

And *another* great bother must be, having to settle *which* leg it had better move first. I think, if *you* had forty or fifty legs, and if you wanted to go a walk, you'd be such a time in settling which leg to begin with, that you'd never go a walk at all!

And what did Alice and the Caterpillar *talk* about, I wonder?

Well, Alice told it how *very* confusing it was, being first one size and then another.

And the Caterpillar asked her if she liked the size she was, just then.

And Alice said she would like to be just a *little* bit larger —— three inches was such a *wretched* height to be! (Just mark off three inches on the wall, about the length of your middle finger, and you'll see what size she was.)

And the Caterpillar told her one side of the mushroom would make her grow *taller*, and the other side would make her grow *shorter*.

So Alice took two little bits of it with her to nibble, and managed to make herself quite a nice comfortable height, before she went on to visit the Duchess.

VIII.

THE PIG-BABY.

Would you like to hear about Alice's visit to the Duchess? It was a very interesting visit indeed, I can assure you.

Of course she knocked at the door to begin with: but nobody came: so she had to open it for herself.

Now, if you look at the picture, you'll see exactly what Alice saw when she got inside.

The door led right into the kitchen, you see. The Duchess sat in the middle of the room, nursing the Baby. The Baby was howling. The soup was boiling. The Cook was stirring the soup. The Cat —— it was a *Cheshire* Cat —— was grinning, as Cheshire Cats always do. All these things were happening just as Alice went in.

The Duchess has a beautiful cap and gown, hasn't she? But I'm afraid she *hasn't* got a very beautiful *face*.

The Baby —— well, I daresay you've seen *several* nicer babies than *that :* and more good-tempered ones, too. However, take a good look at it, and we'll see if you know it again, next time you meet it!

The Cook —— well, you *may* have seen nicer cooks, once or twice.

But I'm nearly sure you've *never* seen a nicer *Cat !* Now *have* you? And *wouldn't* you like to have a Cat of your own, just like that one, with lovely green eyes, and smiling so sweetly?

The Duchess was very rude to Alice. And no wonder. Why, she even called her own *Baby* "Pig!" And it *wasn't* a Pig, *was* it? And she ordered the Cook to chop off Alice's head: though of course the Cook didn't do it: and at last she threw the Baby at her! So Alice caught the Baby, and took it away with her: and I think that was about the best thing she could do.

So she wandered away, through the wood, carrying the ugly little thing with her. And a great job it was to keep hold of it, it wriggled about so. But at last she found out that the *proper* way was, to keep tight hold of its left foot and its right ear.

But don't *you* try to hold on to a Baby like that, my Child! There are not many babies that *like* being nursed in *that* way!

Well, and so the Baby kept grunting, and grunting. so that Alice had to say to it, quite seriously, "If you're going to turn into a *Pig*, my dear, I'll have nothing more to do with you. Mind now!"

And at last she looked down into its face, and what *do* you think had happened to it? Look at the picture, and see if you can guess.

"Why, *that's* not the Baby that Alice was nursing, is it?"

Ah, I *knew* you wouldn't know it again, though I told you to take a good look at it! Yes, it *is* the Baby. And it's turned into a little *Pig!*

So Alice put it down, and let it trot away into the wood. And she said to herself "It was a *very* ugly Baby: but it makes rather a handsome *Pig,* I think."

Don't you think she was right?

IX.

THE CHESHIRE-CAT.

ALL alone, all alone! Poor Alice! No Baby, not even a *Pig* to keep her company!

So you may be sure she was very glad indeed, when she saw the Cheshire-Cat, perched up in a tree, over her head.

The Cat has a very nice smile, no doubt: but just look what a lot of teeth it's got! Isn't Alice just a *little* shy of it?

Well, yes, a *little*. But then, it couldn't help having teeth, you know: and it *could* have helped smiling, supposing it had been cross. So, on the whole, she was *glad*.

Doesn't Alice look very prim, holding her head so straight up, and with her hands behind her, just as if she were going to say her lessons to the Cat!

And that reminds me. There's a little lesson I want to teach *you*, while we're looking at this picture of Alice and the Cat. Now don't be in a bad temper about it, my dear Child! It's a very *little* lesson indeed!

Do you see that Fox-Glove growing close to the tree? And do you know why it's called a *Fox*-Glove? Perhaps you think it's got something to do with a Fox? No indeed! *Foxes* never wear Gloves!

The right word is "*Folk's*-Gloves." Did you ever hear that Fairies used to be called "the good *Folk*"?

Now we've finished the lesson, and we'll wait a minute, till you've got your temper again.

Well? Do you feel quite good-natured again? No temper-ache? No crossness about the corners of the mouth? Then we'll go on.

"Cheshire Puss!" said Alice. (*Wasn't* that a pretty name for a Cat?) "Would you tell me which way I ought to go from here?"

And so the Cheshire-Cat told her which way she ought to go, if she wanted to visit the Hatter, and which way to go, to visit the March Hare. "They're both mad!" said the Cat.

And then the Cat vanished away, just like the flame of a candle when it goes out!

So Alice set off, to visit the March Hare. And as she went along, there was the Cat again! And she told it she didn't *like* it coming and going so quickly.

So this time the Cat vanished quite slowly, beginning with the tail, and ending with the grin. Wasn't *that* a curious thing, a Grin without any Cat ?   Would you like to see one ?

If you turn up the corner of this leaf, you'll have Alice looking at the Grin : and she doesn't look a bit more frightened than when she was looking at the Cat, *does* she ?

X

THE MAD TEA-PARTY.

THIS is the Mad Tea-Party. You see Alice had left the Cheshire-Cat, and had gone off to see the March Hare and the Hatter, as the Cheshire-Cat had advised her : and she found them having tea under a great tree, with a Dormouse sitting between them.

There were only those three at the table, but there were quantities of tea-cups set all along it. You ca'n't see all the table, you know, and even in the bit you *can* see there are nine cups, counting the one the March Hare has got in his hand.

That's the March Hare, with the long ears, and straws mixed up with his hair. The straws

showed he was mad —— I don't know why.
Never twist up straws among *your* hair, for fear
people should think you're mad !

There was a nice green arm-chair at the end
of the table, that looked as if it was just meant
for Alice : so she went and sat down in it.

Then she had quite a long talk with the
March Hare and the Hatter.   The Dormouse
didn't say much.   You see it was fast asleep
generally, and it only just woke up for a
moment, now and then.

As long as it was asleep, it was very useful
to the March Hare and the Hatter, because it
had a nice round soft head, just like a pillow :
so they could put their elbows on it, and lean
across it, and talk to each other quite comfort-
ably.   You wouldn't like people to use *your* head
for a pillow, *would* you ?   But if you were fast
asleep, like the Dormouse, you wouldn't feel it :
so I suppose you wouldn't care about it.

I'm afraid they gave Alice *very* little to eat
and drink.   However, after a bit, she helped
herself to some tea and bread - and - butter : only

I don't quite see where she *got* the bread - and - butter : and she had no plate for it.   Nobody seems to have a plate except the Hatter.   I believe the March Hare must have had one as well : because, when they all moved one place on (that was the rule at this curious tea - party), and Alice had to go into the place of the March Hare, she found he had just up- set the milk - jug into his plate.   So I suppose

his plate and the milk - jug are hidden behind
that large tea - pot.

The Hatter used to carry about hats to sell :
and even the one that he's got on his head is
meant to be sold.   You see it's got its price
marked on it ——— a   10" and a "6" ——— that
means "ten shillings and sixpence."   Wasn't that
a funny way of selling hats ?   And hasn't he got
a beautiful neck - tie on ?   Such a lovely yellow
tie, with large red spots.

He has just got up to say to Alice "Your
hair wants cutting !"   That was a rude thing to
say, *wasn't* it ?   And do you think her hair *does*
want cutting ?   *I* think it's a very pretty length
——— just the right length.

XI.

THE QUEEN'S GARDEN.

THIS is a little bit of the beautiful garden I told you about. You see Alice had managed at last to get quite small, so that she could go through the little door. I suppose she was about as tall as a mouse, if it stood on its hind-legs: so of course this was a *very* tiny rose-tree: and these are *very* tiny gardeners.

What funny little men they are! But *are* they men, do you think? I think they must be live cards, with just a head, and arms, and legs, so as to *look* like little men. And what *are* they doing with that red paint, I wonder? Well, you see, this is what they told Alice

G

The Queen of Hearts wanted to have a *red* rose-
tree just in that corner : and these poor little
gardeners had made a great mistake, and had
put in a *white* one instead : and they were so
frightened about it, because the Queen was *sure*
to be angry, and then she would order all their
heads to be cut off !

She was a dreadfully savage Queen, and that was the way she always did, when she was angry with people. " Off with their heads ! " They didn't *really* cut their heads off, you know : because nobody ever obeyed her : but that was what she always *said*.

Now ca'n't you guess what the poor little gardeners are trying to do ? They're trying to paint the roses *red*, and they're in a great hurry to get it done before the Queen comes. And then *perhaps* the Queen won't find out it was a *white* rose-tree to begin with : and then *perhaps* the little men won't get their heads cut off !

You see there were *five* large white roses on the tree —— such a job to get them all painted red ! But they've got three and a half done, now, and if only they wouldn't stop to talk —— work away, little men, *do* work away ! Or the Queen will be coming before it's done ! And if she finds any *white* roses on the tree, do you know what will happen ? It will be " Off with their heads ! " Oh, work away, my little men ! Hurry, hurry !

The Queen has come!   And *isn't* she angry?
Oh, my poor little Alice!

XII.

THE LOBSTER - QUADRILLE.

DID you ever play at Croquet? There are large wooden balls, painted with different colours, that you have to roll about; and arches of wire, that you have to send them through; and great wooden mallets, with long handles, to knock the balls about with.

Now look at the picture, and you'll see that *Alice* has just been playing a Game of Croquet.

"But she *couldn't* play, with that great red what's-its-name in her arms! Why, how could she hold the mallet?"

Why, my dear Child, that great red what's-its-name (its *real* name is "*a Flamingo*") *is* the mallet! In this Croquet-Game, the balls were

live *Hedge-hogs* —— you know a hedge-hog can
roll itself up into a ball?—— and the mallets
were live *Flamingos!*

So Alice is just resting from the Game, for a
minute, to have a chat with that dear old thing,
the Duchess: and of course she keeps her mallet
under her arm, so as not to lose it.

"But I don't think she *was* a dear old thing, one bit! To call her Baby a *Pig*, and to want to chop off Alice's head!"

Oh, that was only a joke, about chopping off Alice's head: and as to the Baby —— why, it *was* a Pig, you know! And just look at her *smile*! Why, it's wider than all Alice's head: and yet you can only see half of it!

Well, they'd only had a *very* little chat, when the Queen came and took Alice away, to see the Gryphon and the Mock Turtle.

You don't know what a Gryphon is? Well! Do you know *anything?* That's the question. However, look at the picture. That creature with a red head, and red claws, and green scales, is the *Gryphon*. Now you know.

And the other's the *Mock Turtle*. It's got a calf's-head, because calf's-head is used to make *Mock Turtle Soup*. Now you know.

"But what are they *doing*, going round and round Alice like that?"

Why, I thought of *course* you'd know *that!* They're dancing *a Lobster-Quadrille*.

And next time *you* meet a Gryphon and a Mock Turtle, I daresay they'll dance it for *you*, if you ask them prettily. Only don't let them come *quite* close, or they'll be treading on your toes, as they did on poor Alice's.

XIII.

WHO STOLE THE TARTS?

DID you ever hear how the Queen of Hearts made some tarts? And can you tell me what became of them?

"Why, of *course* I can! Doesn't the song tell all about it?

> *The Queen of Hearts, she made some tarts:*
> *All on a summer day:*
> *The Knave of Hearts, he stole those tarts,*
> *And took them quite away!"*

Well, yes, the *Song* says so. But it would never do to punish the poor Knave, just because there was a *Song* about him. They had to take

H

him prisoner, and put chains on his wrists, and bring him before the King of Hearts, so that there might be a regular trial.

Now, if you look at the big picture, at the beginning of this book, you'll see what a grand thing a trial is, when the Judge is a King!

The King is very grand, *isn't* he? But he doesn't look very *happy*. I think that big crown, on the top of his wig, must be *very* heavy and uncomfortable. But he had to wear them *both*, you see, so that people might know he was a Judge *and* a King.

And *doesn't* the Queen look cross? She can see the dish of tarts on the table, that she had taken such trouble to make. And she can see the bad Knave (do you see the chains hanging from his wrists?) that stole them away from her : so I don't think it's any wonder if she *does* feel a *little* cross.

The White Rabbit is standing near the King, reading out the Song, to tell everybody what a bad Knave he is : and the Jury (you can just see two of them, up in the Jury-box, the Frog and the Duck) have to settle whether he's "guilty" or "not guilty."

Now I'll tell you about the accident that happened to Alice.

You see, she was sitting close by the Jury-box: and she was called as a witness. You know what a "witness" is? A "witness" is a person who has seen the prisoner do whatever he's accused of, or at any rate knows *something* that's important in the trial.

But *Alice* hadn't seen the Queen *make* the tarts: and she hadn't seen the Knave *take* the tarts: and, in fact, she didn't know anything about it: so why in the world they wanted *her* to be a witness, I'm sure *I* ca'n't tell you!

Anyhow, they *did* want her. And the White Rabbit blew his big trumpet, and shouted out "Alice!" And so Alice jumped up in a great hurry. And then——

And then what *do* you think happened? Why, her skirt caught against the Jury-box, and tipped it over, and all the poor little Jurors came tumbling out of it!

Let's try if we can make out all the twelve.
You know there ought to be twelve to make up

a Jury. I see the Frog, and the Dormouse, and the Rat and the Ferret, and the Hedgehog, and the Lizard, and the Bantam - Cock, and the Mole, and the Duck, and the Squirrel, and a screaming bird, with a long beak, just behind the Mole.

But that only makes eleven: we must find one more creature.

Oh, do you see a little white head, coming out behind the Mole, and just under the Duck's beak? That makes up the twelve.

Mr. Tenniel says the screaming bird is a *Storkling* (of course you know what *that* is?) and the little white head is a *Mouseling*. Isn't it a little *darling?*

Alice picked them all up again, very carefully, and I hope they weren't *much* hurt!

XIV.

THE SHOWER OF CARDS.

OH dear, oh dear! What *is* it all about? And what's happening to Alice?

Well, I'll tell you all about it, as well I can. The way the trial ended was this. The King wanted the Jury to settle whether the Knave of Hearts was *guilty* or *not guilty* —— that means that they were to settle whether *he* had stolen the Tarts, or if somebody else had taken them. But the wicked *Queen* wanted to have his *punishment* settled, first of all. That wasn't at all fair, *was* it? Because, you know, supposing he never *took* the Tarts, then of course he oughtn't to be punished. Would *you* like to be punished for something you hadn't done?

So Alice said "Stuff and nonsense!"

So the Queen said "Off with her head!" (Just what she always said, when she was angry.)

So Alice said "Who cares for *you?* You're nothing but a pack of cards!"

So they were *all* very angry, and flew up into the air, and came tumbling down again, all over Alice, just like a shower of rain.

And I think you'll *never* guess what happened next. The next thing was, Alice woke up out of her curious dream. And she found that the cards were only some leaves off the tree, that the wind had blown down upon her face.

Wouldn't it be a nice thing to have a curious dream, just like Alice?

The best plan is this. First lie down under a tree, and wait till a White Rabbit runs by, with a watch in his hand: then shut your eyes, and pretend to be dear little Alice.

Good-bye, Alice dear, good-bye!

THE END.

[TURN OVER

AN EASTER GREETING

EVERY CHILD WHO LOVES "ALICE."

My dear Child,

Please to fancy, if you can, that you are reading a real letter, from a real friend whom you have seen, and whose voice you can seem to yourself to hear, wishing you, as I do now with all my heart, a happy Easter.

Do you know that delicious dreamy feeling, when one first wakes on a summer morning, with the twitter of birds in the air, and the fresh breeze coming in at the open window——when, lying lazily with eyes half shut, one sees as in a dream green boughs waving, or waters rippling in a golden light? It is a pleasure very near to sadness, bringing tears to one's eyes like a beautiful picture or poem. And is not that a Mother's gentle hand that undraws your curtains, and a Mother's sweet voice that summons you to rise? To rise and forget, in the bright sunlight, the ugly dreams that frightened you so when all was dark——to rise and enjoy another happy day, first kneeling to thank that unseen Friend who sends you the beautiful sun?

Are these strange words from a writer of such tales as "Alice"? And is this a strange letter to find in a book of nonsense? It may be so. Some perhaps may blame me for thus mixing together things grave and gay; others may smile and think it odd that any one should speak of solemn things at all, except in Church and on a Sunday: but I think——nay, I am sure——that some children will read this gently and lovingly, and in the spirit in which I have written it.

For I do not believe God means us thus to divide life into two halves——to wear a grave face on Sunday, and to think it out-of-place to even so much as mention Him on a week-day. Do you think He cares to see only kneeling figures and to hear only tones of prayer——and that He does not also love to see the lambs leaping in the sunlight, and to hear the merry voices of the children, as they roll among the hay? Surely their innocent laughter is as sweet in His ears as the grandest anthem that ever rolled up from the "dim religious light" of some solemn cathedral?

And if I have written anything to add to those stores of innocent and healthy amusement that are laid up in books for the children *I love so well, it is surely something I may hope to look back upon without shame and sorrow (as how much of life must then be recalled!) when* my *turn comes to walk through the valley of shadows.*

This Easter sun will rise on you, dear child, "feeling your life in every limb," and eager to rush out into the fresh morning air——and many an Easter-day will come and go, before it finds you feeble and grey-headed, creeping wearily out to bask once more in the sunlight——but it is good, even now, to think sometimes of that great morning when "the Sun of righteousness" shall "arise with healing in his wings."

Surely your gladness need not be the less for the thought that you will one day see a brighter dawn than this——when lovelier sights will meet your eyes than any waving trees or rippling waters——when angel-hands shall undraw your curtains, and sweeter tones than ever loving Mother breathed shall wake you to a new and glorious day——and when all the sadness, and the sin, that darkened life on this little earth, shall be forgotten like the dreams of a night that is past!

Your affectionate Friend,

LEWIS CARROLL.

CHRISTMAS GREETINGS.

(FROM A FAIRY TO A CHILD.)

LADY dear, if Fairies may
    For a moment lay aside
Cunning tricks and elfish play,
    'Tis at happy Christmas-tide.

We have heard the children say —
    Gentle children, whom we love —
Long ago, on Christmas Day,
    Came a message from above.

Still, as Christmas-tide comes round,
    They remember it again —
Echo still the joyful sound
    "Peace on earth, good-will to men!"

Yet the hearts must childlike be
    Where such heavenly guests abide:
Unto children, in their glee,
    All the year is Christmas-tide!

Thus, forgetting tricks and play
    For a moment, Lady dear,
We would wish you, if we may,
    Merry Christmas, glad New Year!

LEWIS CARROLL

WORKS BY LEWIS CARROLL.

PUBLISHED BY

MACMILLAN AND CO., LONDON.

ALICE'S ADVENTURES IN WONDERLAND. With Forty-two Illustrations by TENNIEL. (First published in 1865.) Crown 8vo, cloth, gilt edges, price 6s. Eighty-second Thousand.

THE SAME; PEOPLE'S EDITION. (First published in 1887.) Crown 8vo, cloth, price 2s. 6d. Fourteenth Thousand.

AVENTURES D'ALICE AU PAYS DES MERVEILLES. Traduit de l'Anglais par HENRI BUÉ. Ouvrage illustré de 42 Vignettes par JOHN TENNIEL. (First published in 1869.) Crown 8vo, cloth, gilt edges, price 6s. Second Thousand.

Alice's Abenteuer im Wunderland. Aus dem Englischen, von Antonie Zimmermann. Mit 42 Illustrationen von John Tenniel. (First published in 1869.) Crown 8vo, cloth, gilt edges, price 6s.

LE AVVENTURE D'ALICE NEL PAESE DELLE MERAVIGLIE. Tradotte dall' Inglese da T. PIETROCÒLA-ROSSETTI. Con 42 Vignette di GIOVANNI TENNIEL. (First published in 1872.) Crown 8vo, cloth, gilt edges, price 6s.

ALICE'S ADVENTURES UNDER GROUND. Being a Facsimile of the original MS. Book, which was afterwards developed into "Alice's Adventures in Wonderland." With Thirty-seven Illustrations by the Author. (Begun, July, 1862; finished, Feb. 1863; first published, in Facsimile, in 1886.) Crown 8vo, cloth, gilt edges, price 4s. Second Thousand.

THE NURSERY "ALICE." Containing Twenty Coloured Enlargements from TENNIEL'S Illustrations to "Alice's Adventures in Wonderland." With Text adapted to Nursery Readers by LEWIS CARROLL. The Cover designed and coloured by E. GERTRUDE THOMSON. (First published in 1889.) 4to, boards, price 4s.

THROUGH THE LOOKING-GLASS AND WHAT ALICE FOUND THERE. With Fifty Illustrations by TENNIEL. (First published in 1871.) Crown 8vo, cloth, gilt edges, price 6s. Fifty-ninth thousand.

THE SAME; PEOPLE'S EDITION. (First published in 1887.) Crown 8vo, cloth, price 2s. 6d. Ninth Thousand.

ALICE'S ADVENTURES IN WONDERLAND: AND THROUGH THE LOOKING-GLASS; PEOPLE'S EDITIONS. Both Books together in One Volume. (First published in 1887.) Crown 8vo, cloth, price 4s. 6d. Second Thousand.

WORKS BY LEWIS CARROLL.

PUBLISHED BY

MACMILLAN AND CO., LONDON.

THE HUNTING OF THE SNARK. An Agony in Eight Fits. With Nine Illustrations by H. HOLIDAY. (First published in 1876.) Crown 8vo, cloth, large gilt designs on cover, and gilt edges, price 4s. 6d. Eighteenth Thousand.

RHYME? AND REASON? With Sixty-five Illustrations by ARTHUR B. FROST, and Nine by HENRY HOLIDAY. (First published in 1883, being a reprint, with a few additions, of the comic portion of " Phantasmagoria and other Poems," published in 1869, and of "The Hunting of the Snark," published in 1876.) Crown 8vo, cloth, coloured edges, price 6s. Fourth Thousand.

A TANGLED TALE. Reprinted from *The Monthly Packet*. With Six Illustrations by ARTHUR B. FROST. (First published in 1885.) Crown 8vo, cloth, gilt edges, price 4s. 6d. Third Thousand.

THE GAME OF LOGIC. With an Envelope containing a card diagram and nine counters—four red and five grey. (First published in 1886.) Crown 8vo, cloth, price 3s. Second Thousand.
N.B.—The Envelope, etc., may be had separately at 3d. each.

N.B.—In selling Mr. LEWIS CARROLL's books to the Trade, Messrs. MACMILLAN & Co. will abate 2d. in the shilling (no odd copies), and allow 5 per cent. discount for payment within six months, and 10 per cent. for cash. In selling them to the Public (for cash only) they will allow 10 per cent. discount.

Mr. LEWIS CARROLL, having been requested to allow "AN EASTER GREETING" (a leaflet, addressed to children, first published in 1876, and frequently given with his books) to be sold separately, has arranged with Messrs. HARRISON, of 59, Pall Mall, who will supply a single copy for 1d., or 12 for 9d., or 100 for 5s.

CAUTIONS TO READERS.

On August 1st, 1881, a story appeared in *Aunt Judy's Magazine* No. 184, entitled "The Land of Idleness, by LEWIS CARROLL." This story was really written by a lady, FRÄULEIN IDA LACKOWITZ. Acting on her behalf, Mr. CARROLL forwarded it to the Editor : and this led to the mistake of naming him as its author.

In October, 1887, the writer of an article on "Literature for the Little ones," in *The Nineteenth Century*, stated that, in 1864, "TOM HOOD was delighting the world with such works as *From Nowhere to the North Pole*. Between TOM HOOD and Mr. LEWIS CARROLL there is more than a suspicion of resemblance in some particulars. *Alice's Adventures in Wonderland* narrowly escapes challenging a comparison with *From Nowhere to the North Pole*. The idea of both is so similar that Mr. CARROLL can hardly have been surprised if some people have believed he was inspired by HOOD." The date 1864 is a mistake. *From Nowhere to the North Pole* was first published in 1874.

This time Alice waited quietly until it chose to speak again: in a few minutes the caterpillar took the hookah out of its mouth, and got down off the mushroom, and crawled away into the grass, merely remarking as it went: "the top will make you grow taller, and the stalk will make you grow shorter."

"The top of _what_? the stalk of _what_?" thought Alice.

"Of the mushroom," said the caterpillar, just as if she had asked it aloud, and in another moment it was out of sight.

Alice remained looking thoughtfully at the mushroom for a minute, and then picked it and carefully broke it in two,

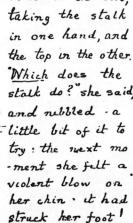

taking the stalk in one hand, and the top in the other. "Which does the stalk do?" she said, and nibbled a little bit of it to try: the next mo -ment she felt a violent blow on her chin: it had struck her foot!

Being a Facsimile of the Original MS. Book, afterwards developed into "Alice's Adventures in Wonderland." With Twenty-seven Illustrations by the Author. Crown 8vo, 4s.

MACMILLAN & CO., LONDON.